Click! Can Cam find a missing car?

"What about my car?" Danny's father asked again.

"I solved that mystery," Jim E. Winter said as he walked into room 17. "I know what happened to your car. Now I have to sign more books."

Jim E. Winter took a hanger from the coatrack. He took off his raincoat and hat and hung them up. Then he turned and faced Danny's father.

"Your car was stolen," Jim E. Winter said. "That's what happened to it. Now you must call the police. And I have to sign more books."

Jim E. Winter quickly left the room.

"Hey," Mr. Pace said. "He didn't solve this mystery. If he did, I would have my car."

Danny turned to Cam. "Now it's up to you," he said. "It's up to you to find my dad's car."

and the Mystery Writer Mystery

by David A. Adler

illustrated by
Joy Allen

PUFFIN BOOKS

PUFFIN BOOKS
Published by the Penguin Group
Penguin Young Readers Group, 345 Hudson Street, New York, New York 10014, U.S.A.
Penguin Group (Canada), 90 Eglinton Avenue East, Suite 700,
Toronto, Ontario, Canada M4P 2Y3 (a division of Pearson Penguin Canada Inc.)
Penguin Books Ltd, 80 Strand, London WC2R 0RL, England
Penguin Ireland, 25 St Stephen's Green, Dublin 2, Ireland (a division of Penguin Books Ltd)
Penguin Group (Australia), 250 Camberwell Road, Camberwell, Victoria 3124, Australia
(a division of Pearson Australia Group Pty Ltd)
Penguin Books India Pvt Ltd, 11 Community Centre,
Panchsheel Park, New Delhi - 110 017, India
Penguin Group (NZ), 67 Apollo Drive, Rosedale, North Shore 0632, New Zealand
(a division of Pearson New Zealand Ltd)
Penguin Books (South Africa) (Pty) Ltd, 24 Sturdee Avenue,
Rosebank, Johannesburg 2196, South Africa

Registered Offices: Penguin Books Ltd, 80 Strand, London WC2R 0RL, England

First published in the United States of America by Viking,
a division of Penguin Young Readers Group, 2007
Published by Puffin Books, a division of Penguin Young Readers Group, 2008

1 3 5 7 9 10 8 6 4 2

Text copyright © David A. Adler, 2007
Illustrations copyright © Joy Allen, 2007
All rights reserved

THE LIBRARY OF CONGRESS HAS CATALOGED THE VIKING EDITION AS FOLLOWS:
Adler, David A.
Cam Jansen and the mystery writer mystery / by David A. Adler ;
illustrated by Joy Allen.
p. cm.
Summary: Cam Jansen battles a famous children's mystery writer
to see who can solve the case of the stolen car.
ISBN 978-0-670-06199-0 (hc)
[1. Authors—Fiction. 2. Crime—Fiction. 3. Mystery and detective stories.]
I. Allen, Joy, ill. II. Title.
PZ7.A2615Cap 2007
[Fic]—dc22 2006102020

Puffin Books ISBN 978-0-14-241194-0

Printed in the United States of America

Set in New Baskerville

Except in the United States of America, this book is sold subject to the condition that
it shall not, by way of trade or otherwise, be lent, re-sold, hired out, or otherwise
circulated without the publisher's prior consent in any form of binding or cover
other than that in which it is published and without a similar condition
including this condition being imposed on the subsequent purchaser.

The publisher does not have any control over and does not assume
any responsibility for author or third-party Web sites or their content.

For Tzvi Lewisohn,
my neighbor with the great story ideas
—D.A.

To my grandson Curt, a great reader
and friend, who takes me on many
adventurous trails and mysteries
—J.A.

BOOK FAIR
#1MOM

Chapter One

"'I can solve it!' Barry Blake says at the start of each book. 'I can solve any mystery.' He's so smart," Cam Jansen told her mother. "He's strong, too. He once lifted the front of a truck just to find a clue."

"Yes," Mrs. Jansen said. "But do you remember what else he always says? 'I can solve any mystery and be home in time to help Mom with dinner.' He's a very good son."

It was a cold, rainy December night. Cam and her mother were on their way to school. It was the night of the yearly book fair. Jim E. Winter, the author of Cam's favorite books, the My Name Is Blake Mysteries, would be there.

"It's so difficult to drive in this weather," Mrs. Jansen said, and leaned forward. "With all this rain and the cold, it's hard to see out. The car windows are all fogged up."

Cam's mother was stopped at a traffic light. She took a tissue and wiped the inside of the front window.

"Did you ever see a picture of Jim E. Winter?" she asked Cam.

"Yes. There's one on the back of each of his books."

"I bet there's no fog on your memory," Mrs. Jansen said. "Tell me what he looks like."

Cam closed her eyes. She said, *"Click!"* Then Cam said, "I'm looking at a picture of Jim E. Winter. He's really young. He has a dark bushy mustache and lots of dark wavy hair."

The light changed to green.

Mrs. Jansen drove slowly.

Cam said, "In the picture he's wearing a polka-dotted bow tie and a striped shirt."

Cam has what people call a photographic memory. She remembers just about everything she's seen. It's as if she has a camera and a file of pictures in her head.

Cam said, *"Click!"* again.

"On the cover beneath the picture," Cam

said with her eyes still closed, "is lots of information. It says, 'Jim E. Winter was once a police detective. He's written more than one hundred books. He lives near a forest and has a dog named Jake.'"

When Cam wants to remember something she's seen, she closes her eyes and says, *"Click!"* Cam says it's the sound her mental camera makes.

Cam's real name is Jennifer, but when people found out about her amazing memory, they called her "The Camera." Soon "The Camera" became just "Cam."

Mrs. Jansen was just about to turn onto the school's front drive. "We're finally here!" Mrs. Jansen said. "And I'm glad. It's not easy driving in this rain."

Cam opened her eyes.

"Mom! Be careful!" Cam said. "Someone is walking just ahead."

Mrs. Jansen stepped on the car's brakes. She waited for the man to cross the road. Then she drove past the front of the school to the side parking lot.

"Button your coat," Mrs. Jansen told Cam when she stopped the car. "Put on your rain hat."

Mrs. Jansen took an umbrella from the backseat. She opened it. Then she and Cam hurried into the school.

There was a large mat by the door. Cam and her mother wiped their shoes.

A sign directed them to hang their coats in room 17. Mrs. Jansen closed her umbrella. She and Cam hung their coats, hats, and umbrella in room 17.

Beth Kane and her father were in the room, too.

"Hi, Cam," Beth said.

"Hello," Beth's father said, and shook Cam's hand. "It's nice to see you again."

Cam smiled. "Thanks."

Mr. Kane shook Mrs. Jansen's hand.

"Your daughter is amazing," he said. "You must be so proud of her."

Mrs. Jansen smiled. "And Cam has told me how nice and smart Beth is."

Then, as they were about to leave room

17, Danny and his parents entered the school.

"Hey, there's Cam Jansen," Danny told his parents. "She's the *clicking* girl. And there's Beth. She's the girl who never likes my jokes."

Beth told Danny, "No one likes your jokes."

"Hey," Danny's father said. "I'm Mr. Pace, and you'll like my jokes. Here's one: What do you get from nervous hens?"

"I know that one," Danny said, and laughed. "The answer is 'scrambled eggs.'" Then Danny asked his father, "Do you know Snow White's father's name? It's Egg White. Now the yolk is on you, Dad. Do you get it? The *yolk* is on you."

"That's enough jokes," Danny's mother said. "Let's just hang up our coats."

"Wow," Beth said as she, Cam, and their parents walked into the hall. "Danny's father tells bad jokes, too."

"Welcome," Dr. Prell, the school's principal, said. "We have books for everyone. The book fair is in the gym."

The doors to the gym were open. Cam, Beth, and their parents went in. They stood there for a moment and looked at the many tables. On each was a pile of books and a sign so people would know what kind of books were on the table.

"I'm looking for history books," Mrs.

Jansen told Cam. "You can look by yourself, but please don't leave this room."

"I want to meet Jim E. Winter," Cam said.

Beth said, "Me, too. I love his mysteries."

"Stay with Cam," Mr. Kane told his daughter. "I'm going to look at the biographies."

Children and their parents were looking at books. There were small children, too, running between and under the tables.

"There he is," Beth said, and pointed. "He's in the back of the gym, right by the wall."

Cam looked across the gym. An old bald man with a white bushy mustache was sitting by a table at the far end of the gym. A long line of children were waiting for him to sign their books.

"That man is bald! That can't be Jim E. Winter," Cam said. "I saw a picture of him with dark, wavy hair and a dark mustache."

Beth said, "You must have looked at an old picture of him."

"Yes," Cam said. "It must have been a *very* old picture."

Cam looked at the many people waiting to meet Jim E. Winter. Each had a My Name Is Blake Mystery for him to sign.

"Well," Cam said, "I don't care what he looks like. I don't care how old he is. I just want to meet him."

Chapter Two

"I'm getting Jim E. Winter's newest mystery," Cam said. "I want him to sign it. Then I want to read it."

Cam looked at the many tables and signs in the gym. There were tables with easy-to-read books, biographies, cookbooks, mysteries, other fiction, and riddle and joke books. Danny and his father were at the riddles and jokes table.

There was a table in the middle of the gym with books by Jim E. Winter. That's where Cam and Beth went.

Many children and their parents were

there. Cam and Beth had to wait to get close to the table.

Beth picked up a book. "This is number twenty-seven, *My Name Is Blake and the Scary Movie Mystery,*" Beth said. "It's the newest one."

Cam took a copy of *The Scary Movie Mystery.* Then she found a copy of Jim E. Winter's first book, *My Name Is Blake and the Diamond Rattle Mystery,* and took that, too.

"Hey," Danny said, "look at all the joke books I found."

He had four books. His mother, Mrs. Pace, was with him.

"My dad has even more," Danny said, and pushed close to the table. "Now I'm getting a Jim E. Winter book."

Cam found another Jim E. Winter book she had not read. Now she had three books. She went to the end of the line to get her books signed. The line went down the middle of the gym. Beth, Danny, and Danny's mother got on line right behind Cam.

"This is a long line," Danny said, "and I

know just what to do so we don't get bored waiting. I'll tell jokes."

"Please don't," Beth told him.

"Danny," Mrs. Pace said, "save the jokes for Dad. He likes them."

Danny opened a joke book. He read a joke and laughed. "Are you sure you don't want me to tell you this one? It's really funny."

"Yes," Beth said. "I'm sure."

"We'll look for Eric," Cam said. "That's

what we'll do while we wait. He told me he would be here. I know he wants to meet Jim E. Winter."

Cam looked across the gym. It was crowded. Lots of people were looking at books. Cam's mother was still standing by the history table. She was holding an open book and reading it. Beth's father was by the biography table.

"There he is," Beth said. "Eric is by the easy-to-read table. One of his sisters is with him, but I'm not sure which one."

Eric has twin sisters, Donna and Diane.

Cam waved to Eric. He saw her and waved back.

Danny's father came over. He was holding a large stack of books. "Give me your joke books," he told Danny. "I'll pay for them and put them in the car. Then we can get more."

Danny gave him his joke books.

"Waiting is boring," Beth complained. "This line isn't even moving."

"Yes it is," Danny said. "The back of the

line is moving. It's getting longer. Even more people are waiting to get their books signed."

Some children from the front of the line walked past.

"He wrote, 'Happy Reading, Virginia,'" one of the children said. "He signed it, 'Detective James E. Winter.'"

Cam and everyone behind her took a few steps forward.

Cam said, "If we read our books while we wait, we won't be bored."

Cam opened *My Name Is Blake and the Scary Movie Mystery.* She started to read it to herself.

In the first chapter, Barry Blake is waiting on a long line, too. He and his mother are waiting to see a scary movie. Then, just as they are about to buy tickets, a woman comes to the ticket office.

"Someone stole my purse," the woman in the book says. "I was watching the movie and someone stole it."

"Don't worry," Barry Blake tells her. "I'll

find your purse. I'll solve this mystery. I'll solve it fast and be back in time to see the movie. After the movie, I'll go home in time to help my mom prepare dinner."

In the second chapter, Barry Blake walks into the theater. The woman shows him where she was sitting.

The people on line ahead of Cam moved up. Cam and the others moved one step closer to Jim E. Winter.

"I'm still bored," Beth said, and closed her book. "What's taking so long?"

Cam stepped off the line. She looked at the table.

"He's not just signing books," Cam told Beth and Danny. "He's talking to people. He's posing for pictures."

Eric, his sister Diane, and their father walked over.

"Hi," Eric said. "Are you waiting for Jim Winter?"

"No," Beth told him. "We're waiting for Jim *E.* Winter. Don't forget the *E*!"

The line moved again. Cam and the others took a few steps forward. Now they could hear Jim E. Winter. He thanked a girl for reading his books.

"What is your name?" he asked.

"Gina," the girl answered.

Jim E. Winter signed her book.

Cam and the others took one more step forward. It was their turn to meet the author.

Just then Danny's father came back. He was wearing his raincoat and carrying an umbrella. Both were wet. He was also carrying a large bag of books. He hurried to the front of the line.

"It's gone," he told his wife and Danny. "I paid for the books. Then I went outside to put them in the car, and the car was gone!"

Chapter Three

"Is this a joke?" Mrs. Pace asked.

"No," Danny's father answered. "It's not a joke. I went to where I parked the car, and it's not there."

"You stay here with Danny," Mrs. Pace said, and took the umbrella. "I'm going out to check."

Mrs. Pace walked quickly out of the gym. Mr. Pace stood there. Water dripped off his raincoat.

"This is exciting," Jim E. Winter said. "This is just the sort of mystery I like to solve. Please, tell me what happened."

"I went to put these books in my car," Danny's father told Mr. Winter, "but my car was gone. I had parked it on the side of the school between a yellow van and a white car. I wouldn't forget that. I have a good memory."

"You may have a good memory," Eric said, "but Cam has the best memory. She can say, '*Click!*' and remember everything. She can say, '*Click!*' and solve any mystery."

"Maybe she does have a good memory," Jim E. Winter said, and stood up. "But I was once a police detective."

"Go on," Eric told Cam. "Say, '*Click!*' Prove to Mr. Winter that you remember everything you've seen."

Cam looked at Jim E. Winter. She stepped to the side, turned to face the wall, and closed her eyes. Cam said, "*Click!*

"You're wearing a blue shirt," Cam said with her eyes still closed. "There are two pens in your shirt pocket and a red stain just under the second button."

"That's tomato sauce," Mr. Winter said. "I ate spaghetti for dinner." Mr. Winter turned to Danny's father and asked, "Are you sure you remember where you parked your car?"

"Yes," he answered. "The parking spots are numbered. My car was in number thirty-six. I just went outside, and spot number thirty-six is empty."

Cam was still facing the wall. Her eyes were still closed. "You're wearing blue jeans," she said, "and cowboy boots."

"Isn't she amazing?" Eric asked.

No one answered.

Mr. Winter took a sheet of paper from the table. He took a pen from his shirt pocket. "Please," he said to Mr. Pace, "describe your car."

Cam opened her eyes.

"It's dark blue," Danny's father said. "It has four doors and it looks like any other car. It has two big round lights in front, and lots of windows."

Mr. Winter wrote the description on the paper.

"Do you remember the license-plate number?"

"There's a *G* in it, and an *E*," Danny's father answered. "There's a seven and some other numbers. I don't remember them all, but I can check. My car registration is in my wallet."

"Ha!" Mr. Winter said. "It's just as I thought.

You're not very good with numbers! Maybe the car was not in spot thirty-six. Maybe it was spot sixty-three or thirty-three or sixty-six."

"No. It was in thirty-six."

Eric asked Cam, "Do you remember if their car was in that spot?"

"They came after us," Cam said. "We were leaving the coatroom when they came in. I didn't see their car."

Just then Mrs. Pace returned to the gym. Water dripped from her closed umbrella and raincoat. She walked to the head of the line.

"I checked," she told her husband. "You're right. The car is gone."

"Don't worry," Mr. Winter said. "I'll find your car."

"No," Eric said. "Cam will find it. She'll just say, *'Click!'* and solve the mystery."

"'*Click! Click!*' You keep saying that. Hey, wait. All those *clicks* gives me an idea," Jim E. Winter said. He stepped around the table. He stood right by Danny's father. "I may have already solved this mystery." Mr. Winter held his hand in front of Danny's father and said, "Let me see your car keys."

Mr. Pace reached into the right pocket of his raincoat. Then he reached into his left pocket and took out his keys. He gave them to Jim E. Winter.

"Look at this," Mr. Winter said. "You have a clicker on your key chain. I don't need to know where you parked your car. All I have to do is go to the parking lot and press this clicker. The lights on one of the cars will flash or the horn will honk. And that will be your car."

There was still a long line of people waiting to get their books signed.

"I'll be right back," Mr. Winter said. "I'll sign all your books. But first, I'll solve this mystery."

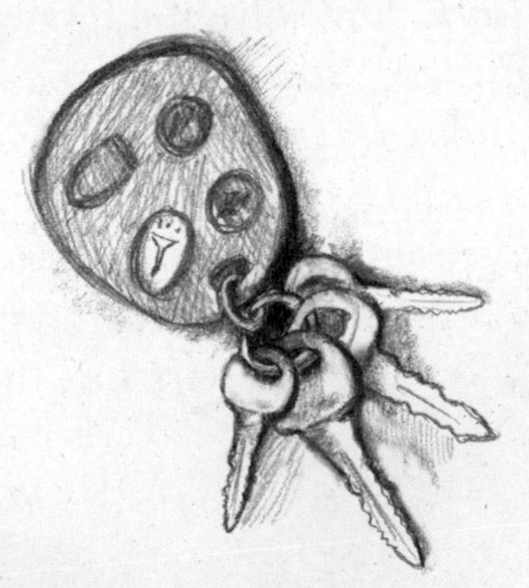

Chapter Four

"This is so exciting," Beth said. "I'm going out. I want to be there when Jim E. Winter solves this mystery."

Eric said, "I'm going, too."

"I have to do something with these books," Cam said. "I didn't pay for them. I can't take them out of the gym."

"And I have to get my dad," Beth said. "I'll have to tell him I'm going outside."

Cam and the other children put their books on a table near the entrance. Beth got her dad. Then Cam, Eric, Diane, Danny, Beth, and their parents all followed Jim

E. Winter out of the gym. They followed him to room 17 for their coats, hats, and umbrellas.

"Button your coat. Put on your rain hat," Mrs. Jansen told Cam. "I don't want you to get sick."

Jim E. Winter put on a large dark-blue raincoat and an old felt hat. He bent down the front brim of his hat and walked outside.

Cam and all the others followed him.

"Look, Mom," Cam whispered. "There's our car."

"Oh, good," Mrs. Jansen told Cam.

Danny's father pointed to parking spot thirty-six and said, "My car was right there, and now it's gone."

"Well," Mr. Winter told him, "that part of your story checks out. There's no car in thirty-six. But I think you got your numbers mixed." He smiled. "I don't need to know where you think your car was. This clicker will find it."

Mr. Winter held the clicker out and pressed it as he walked through the side parking lot. No lights blinked. No horn honked.

Cam and the others followed him.

Mr. Winter walked to the lot behind the building. He kept pressing the clicker, but still, no lights blinked. No horn honked.

A gust of wind blew Mr. Winter's hat off.

He ran and grabbed it. He shook the water off the hat and put it on.

"This is a terrible night to be outside," he complained. "It's so windy. It's so cold and wet."

The parking lot was dark. The only people outside were those looking for Danny's father's car.

"Here," Jim E. Winter said, and gave Danny's father his keys. "I have books to sign. I'm going inside."

Cam watched Mr. Pace take the keys. As he put them in the pocket of his raincoat, Cam looked at him, blinked her eyes, and said, *"Click!"*

"But what about my car?" Danny's father asked. "You said you would find it."

Danny's father ran after Mr. Winter. Danny, his mother, Cam, and some of the others followed the two men into the school.

"What about my car?" Danny's father asked again.

"I solved that mystery," Jim E. Winter said as he walked into room 17. "I know what happened to your car. Now I have to sign more books."

Jim E. Winter took a hanger from the coatrack. He took off his raincoat and hat and hung them up. Then he turned and faced Danny's father.

"Your car was stolen," Jim E. Winter said. "That's what happened to it. Now you must call the police. And I have to sign more books."

Jim E. Winter quickly left the room.

"Hey," Mr. Pace said. "He didn't solve this mystery. If he did, I would have my car."

Danny turned to Cam. "Now it's up to you," he said. "It's up to you to find my dad's car."

Chapter Five

Danny's father took out a cell phone. He pressed some of the buttons, waited, and then said, "My car has been stolen."

Mr. Pace described his car and gave the address of the school.

He listened.

"Thank you," he said. "I'll wait for you in the front lobby."

He returned the cell phone to his pocket. Danny and his parents left room 17. Cam was about to follow them.

"Hang up your coat and hat," Mrs. Jansen told Cam. "I don't want you wearing your wet things."

Cam hung up her coat and hat. Then she followed Danny and his parents to the lobby.

"My car was stolen from the school parking lot," Danny's father told Dr. Prell. "The police are coming."

"That's terrible," Dr. Prell said. "I'll wait here with you. I'll do whatever I can to help."

"I'll help, too," Cam said.

"Please," the principal told Cam, "go back to the gym. The police will handle this."

"I agree with Dr. Prell," Mrs. Jansen told Cam. "When it's all over, Danny will tell us what happened."

Mrs. Jansen walked with Cam into the gym. Beth and her dad went, too. Cam and Beth took their books from the table near the entrance to the gym.

"Let's get back on line and have our books signed," Beth said.

"You go ahead," Cam said. "I'll wait here. I want to see what happens."

"Stay right here," Mrs. Jansen told her. "I don't want you bothering Dr. Prell."

Beth got on line to have her books signed.

Her father went back to the biography table. Cam's mother returned to the history book table.

Cam stood by the entrance to the gym. She looked through the open doors and waited.

Danny and his parents stood in the lobby with Dr. Prell. Cam could see that they were talking, but she couldn't hear what they were saying. Two police officers walked into the school. Cam watched them talk to Dr. Prell and Danny's parents.

Hey, Cam thought, *I know one of those officers. He's been at the school before. That's Officer Oppen.*

Cam waved to him. She hoped he would see her and ask her to come into the lobby. *If a police officer tells me to leave the gym,* Cam thought, *I'll have to go!*

Officer Oppen had his police pad out. He was writing whatever Danny's father said.

Danny's father reached into his pocket. He took out his wallet and showed something to Officer Oppen.

That must be information on his car, Cam thought.

Cam waved some more. She called out, "Hello!"

Officer Oppen saw Cam. He smiled, but he didn't tell her to join him.

Danny's father talked some more. Then it seemed he was done. Officer Oppen closed his pad.

Just then, Eric, his sister Diane, and his father came into the school. They hurried over to the police officers. Mr. Shelton said something, and Officer Oppen took out his pad again. He started to write.

Cam waved to Eric. He didn't see her. Cam called out his name.

Eric looked toward the gym. He saw Cam. He waved to her. Then he held up his hand. He would be right there.

Cam waited and watched. Officer Oppen wrote a lot in his pad. Then Mr. Shelton took out his wallet and showed something to Officer Oppen.

Cam waved again to Eric. She signaled to him to come over.

Eric hurried to the gym entrance.

"You won't believe what happened," he told Cam. "After all of you went inside, Dad said, 'Hey, where's *my* car?' We looked and looked, but it's gone. My dad's car was stolen, too!"

Chapter Six

"Two cars were stolen from the school lot," Cam said. "I have to tell Mom."

"Wait," Eric said. "First listen to what the police officer told us. He said he would call in the license number and description of our car. The police will look for it. But he said they may not find Dad's car."

"Wow!"

"Dad's dry-cleaning—a few shirts and his good suit—is in the trunk. Donna's and Diane's ice skates are also in the trunk."

"Wait here," Cam said. "I'll tell Mom what happened. She said I have to stay in the gym, but I can't stay here with so much happening outside."

"I'll go with you," Eric said. "I'll tell her we need you to find Dad's car."

Cam and Eric went to the history book table.

"Look at this," Mrs. Jansen said to them. "This book is all about Benjamin Franklin. Did you know he made the first bifocal eye-glasses?"

"Mom," Cam said, "Mr. Shelton's car was stolen. I want to help look for it."

"Oh, my," Mrs. Jansen said to Eric. "Your father should call the police."

"He already spoke with the police. They said they'll do what they can."

Mrs. Jansen told Eric, "We can give you a ride home."

"Please," Cam said. "Maybe I can help find the car. Let me go with Eric."

Mrs. Jansen returned the book about Benjamin Franklin to the table.

"I'll go with you," she told Cam. "I'll make

sure you don't do anything dangerous. And if you go outside, I want to be sure your put on your raincoat and hat."

Cam returned her three My Name Is Blake mysteries to the table by the entrance to the gym.

Jim E. Winter walked past them. "I'm finished," he told Dr. Prell. "There's no one left on line."

The principal introduced the writer to Officers Gray and Oppen.

"I read your books when I was a child," Officer Gray said.

"I read them to my children now," Officer Oppen told Mr. Winter.

Officer Gray was a tall woman with curly black hair. Officer Oppen was not so tall and had a short beard.

Cam, Eric, and Mrs. Jansen joined them.

"Hello," Officer Oppen said to Cam. Then he laughed, blinked his eyes, and said, "*Click!*"

"I know this girl," he told his partner. "She's smart. She has a great memory."

"That's very nice," the taller officer said. "But we must get going."

Officer Gray reached into her pocket and took out a set of car keys.

"Are you left-handed?" Cam asked.

"Yes, I am, but how did you know?"

"You keep your keys in your left pocket," Cam explained.

"That's very interesting," Officer Gray said, "but we really must go."

Cam closed her eyes. She said, *"Click!"* Then, with her eyes still closed, she said, "And, Mr. Pace, are you right-handed?"

"Yes, I am," Danny's father said.

"I know that," Cam said with her eyes still closed, "because when Jim E. Winter asked for your keys, you first reached into your right pocket."

"But the keys weren't there," Mr. Pace said.

"No," Cam said. "They were in your left pocket."

"Right pocket, left pocket!" Officer Gray said. "Let's go. We have reports to file."

Cam opened her eyes.

"You're right-handed," Cam told Danny's father, "so you would have put your keys in your right pocket. But I think someone took your keys out of your pocket and then put them back."

"The thief?" Mr. Pace asked.

"Yes," Cam said. "I think he took off your car key. Then he put the keys back. He used the key to steal your car."

Mr. Pace took his keys out of his right pocket. There were several keys on his key ring. He checked them all.

"You're right," he said. "My car key *is* missing."

Mr. Shelton took out his key ring and looked at it. "Hey," he said. "My car key is also missing."

"What does all this mean?" Jim E. Winter asked.

"It means," Cam said, "that the thief came into the school. He went into room seventeen, stole the keys, and then stole the cars."

Chapter Seven

Officer Oppen took out his pad. Jim E. Winter took out a pad, too.

"I've got to write all this down," Officer Oppen said.

"I'll tell you what happened," Cam said. "I remembered that Danny's father first reached into one raincoat pocket and then the other to get his keys. That told me two things. First, he kept his keys in his raincoat, which he left in room seventeen. Anyone who went into the coatroom could take his keys."

"I know what's second," Eric said. "Someone must have moved his keys from one pocket to the other. Since his car was stolen, it must have been the thief."

Jim E. Winter wrote all this in his pad. "This is clever, very clever," he said as he wrote. "I can use this in one of my books."

"But how did he know which coats to search?" Officer Gray asked.

"He was somewhere in the parking lot," Cam said. "He watched people as they got out of their cars. If he saw someone put his keys in his coat pocket, he remembered the coat and stole the keys."

"He didn't even have to remember the coat," Officer Oppen said. "He just went to room seventeen and checked which raincoat was still dripping wet. That meant it was just hung up." Officer Oppen closed his pad. "I told you this girl is smart," he said to Officer Gray.

"Okay, she's smart," Officer Gray said. "We know how the thief stole the cars. But we still don't know where to find him."

"You also don't know where to find my car," Mr. Pace said.

"Or mine," Mr. Shelton added.

"We do know something else," Jim E. Winter said. "He came back after he stole the first car, so he must have left it nearby. Maybe it's hidden somewhere."

"Yes!" Officer Gray said. "Let's drive around. If he's anywhere near this school, we'll find him."

The two police officers started to walk toward the front door of the school.

Cam closed her eyes. She said, *"Click!"*

"Wait!" Eric called out. "Cam is looking at another picture. She may have another clue."

The two police officers stopped. They turned and waited.

"I think I saw him," Cam said with her eyes still closed. "I think I saw the thief."

"Where did you go?" Cam's mother asked her. "I told you to stay in the gym."

"Mom, we both saw him. When you drove

into the school parking lot, you had to stop. A man was walking across the road."

"Yes, of course," Mrs. Jansen said. "Who else but a thief would be walking in such horrible weather?"

Officer Oppen had his pad out again. "Can you describe him?" he asked.

"The car windows were fogged," Cam said. "But I did see that he was short and fat. I saw his raincoat, too. It was light brown. He had on a large brown hat."

"Oh, I also saw him!" Dr. Prell said. "The brim of his hat was bent over his eyes, so I didn't see his face. But I saw him. He came in and said his daughter was already inside. I told him where to hang his coat and where the books were."

Dr. Prell shook her head. "I even welcomed him to the book fair!"

"Well, we'll catch him," Officer Gray said. "We'll catch him and welcome him to jail."

Officers Gray and Oppen left the school.

"That was great!" Jim E. Winter said. "I

might put a girl like you in one of my next mysteries. She'll have red hair and freckles just like yours. I'll name her Camelia."

"'Cam' is not short for 'Camelia,'" Eric said. "It's short for 'The Camera.' We call her that because she has a mental camera. Her real name is Jennifer."

"Oh, yes," Jim E. Winter said, and wrote in his pad.

Cam stood by the front door to the school. She watched the police drive off in their car.

"Good," Cam said. "Now that the police car is gone, maybe we can catch the thief."

With her hands, Cam wiped the fog off the school's large front window.

"Look at your hands," Cam's mother told her. "They're all wet!"

Cam wiped her hands on her shirt.

"Look at your shirt," Mrs. Jansen said. "Now that's wet."

"I'm sorry," Cam said. "But I want to see out the window. Before, the police car was here. That would scare the thief away. But now it's gone. The thief already came here twice to steal. Maybe he'll try again. If he does, we'll see him, and we'll catch him."

Chapter Eight

"So," Eric asked Cam, "what do we do? How do we catch the thief?"

"We wait here and watch for him," Cam said.

"Much of detective work is waiting and watching," Jim E. Winter told Eric. He looked around. "But when I was a detective, I usually did my watching sitting down."

There was a bench near the entrance. Mr. Winter pulled the bench to the window and sat on it.

"You know," Jim E. Winter said, "the thief may not come back. He may have room in his garage for only two cars. Or he may have come back and seen the police car. That would have scared him away."

"I'm waiting," Danny said, "and the crook won't show up. That's not right."

"Lots of times," Mr. Winter told him, "when I was a detective, I waited and watched and nothing happened."

Danny whispered to Cam, "I could tell jokes. Then waiting here would be fun."

Cam shook her head and whispered, "No. Waiting for a thief is too serious for jokes."

"I have a question," Eric said. "Why did the thief take the car key off the ring? He could have just taken all the keys."

Jim E. Winter smiled.

"I have two answers to your question. It could be that he thought if he left the key ring, it would take longer for your dad and that other dad to know something was wrong. They would find their keys. They would not know their cars were stolen until later, when they went outside."

Cam wiped the fog off the window again. Mrs. Jansen quickly gave Cam tissues. She didn't want Cam to wipe her hands on her shirt.

"What's the other reason?" Eric asked.

"Oh, the other reason," Jim E. Winter said, and laughed. "Crooks often do strange things. That's because they're usually not the smartest people. If they were smart, they wouldn't be stealing. In the end, they always get caught."

"Cam, there you are," someone called.

Cam turned. It was Beth.

"I was looking everywhere for you," she said. "Look at my books. Mr. Winter signed them."

Jim E. Winter turned.

"Oh," Beth said. "I didn't know you were here."

"I chose three of your books," Cam told Mr. Winter. "I'll go in right now and pay for them. Then will you sign them for me?"

"Of course I will."

Cam and her mother returned to the gym. Mrs. Jansen paid for the books. Then Cam brought them to Mr. Winter.

"Did anything happen?" Cam asked Eric.

"No. Just that the window fogged up again and I wiped it."

Jim E. Winter looked at Cam and smiled. Then he signed the books, *For Cam, a smart detective, from Detective Jim E. Winter.*

"Thank you," Cam said.

Cam looked outside. A car entered the school parking lot.

"Look," Cam whispered. "If the thief is here, he'll be watching, too. Maybe he'll try to steal this car."

Cam and the others watched the driver and his daughter get out of the car. The driver put the keys in his raincoat pocket. He opened an umbrella. Then he walked with his daughter into the school.

No one followed him.

"Welcome to the book fair," Dr. Prell told the man and his daughter. "Please hang your coats in room seventeen. And please don't leave your keys in your coat pocket. The books are in the gym."

Everyone was quiet after that. They waited and watched.

Cam opened her copy of *My Name Is Blake and the Scary Movie Mystery.*

Cam turned to the third chapter. In it, Barry Blake is in the theater. He's looking for the woman's purse.

You won't find it, Cam thought. *That woman forgot where she was sitting. She's taking you to the wrong seat.*

Cam kept reading. In the fourth chapter, Barry Blake asks the woman if she is sure she brought her purse to the theater.

"Of course I did," she says. "I had to buy a ticket, didn't I? Well, I paid for it with some of the money I keep in my purse."

A mother and her two sons walked past

Cam and the others. They left the school. Cam watched them go to the parking lot. The woman found her car and drove off.

Cam read some more. In chapter six, Barry Blake finds the woman's purse. No one had taken it. The woman had just forgotten where she had been sitting.

I knew it, Cam thought.

Cam closed the book.

Just then, three police cars drove up. Officer Oppen got out of the first car and entered the school.

"We drove up and down every block near the school," he said. "We looked in every driveway, and then we saw a garage with the lights on. We looked in the window, and there they were—the two stolen cars."

"I bet that garage has an automatic electric eye," Jim E. Winter said. "When you go in or out, the light goes on."

"Yes," Officer Oppen said. "We found a man in the garage and arrested him. He's outside." Then he said to Cam, "We need you to tell us if he's the man you saw in the parking lot."

"I don't want my daughter to meet any thief," Mrs. Jansen told the officer. "He might be dangerous."

"He's handcuffed," Officer Oppen said. "We'll take him out of the car. We'll shine a big light on him. You'll be able to see him. But don't worry. The light will be shining in his eyes. He won't be able to see you."

"Well," Mrs. Jansen said, "that sounds safe."

Cam joined Officers Oppen and Gray by the door to the school. Officer Oppen held a large light. He pointed it at a short fat man in a light-brown raincoat. Two police officers were standing beside him.

Cam closed her eyes. She said, *"Click!"* She looked at the picture she had in her head of the man in the parking lot.

"Yes," Cam said, and opened her eyes. "That's him."

"Thank you," Officer Oppen said. He

BOOK

waved to the other officers to let them know that Cam identified the thief.

"I'm sorry," the short man in the light-brown raincoat called out as he got into the back of the first police car.

The police car drove off.

Cam and the two officers went back into the school.

"These are yours," Officer Gray said. She gave a car key to Mr. Shelton and another to Mr. Pace. "We'll take you to your cars."

"This is a story with a happy ending," Jim E. Winter said. "It's happy for everyone but the thief. People will get their cars back, and I've got a great idea for a new book."

"You're going to put this in a book?" Eric asked.

"Yes, and in the front of the book I'll thank Cam Jansen for helping me solve the mystery."

"He didn't solve the mystery," Eric whispered to Cam. "You solved it all by yourself."

"I don't care about that," Cam Jansen said. "What I care about is that my name will be in a book. Isn't that great? My name will be in a book!"

A Cam Jansen Memory Game

Take another look at the picture opposite page 1. Study it. Blink your eyes and say, "*Click!*" Then turn back to this page and answer these questions. Please, first study the picture, *then* look at the questions.

1. Is it raining in the picture?
2. How many cars are in the picture? How many open umbrellas?
3. What is written on the sign above the school doors?
4. How many school windows are in the picture? Is anyone looking out?
5. Is anyone in the picture wearing a skirt?